the Bowling Pin

ISBN: 1502382547

ISBN-13: 978-1502382542

CreateSpace Independent Publishing Platform,

North Charleston, SC.
Printed in the United States of America.

This book was written because of
how badly I long to bowl strikes,
but can't because of that
one lone, aggravating pin...
Pinny.

This goes out to all those
who have been in that situation,
and to those who refuse
to give up on their dreams.

This is Johnny. He almost bowled a strike!

Except...

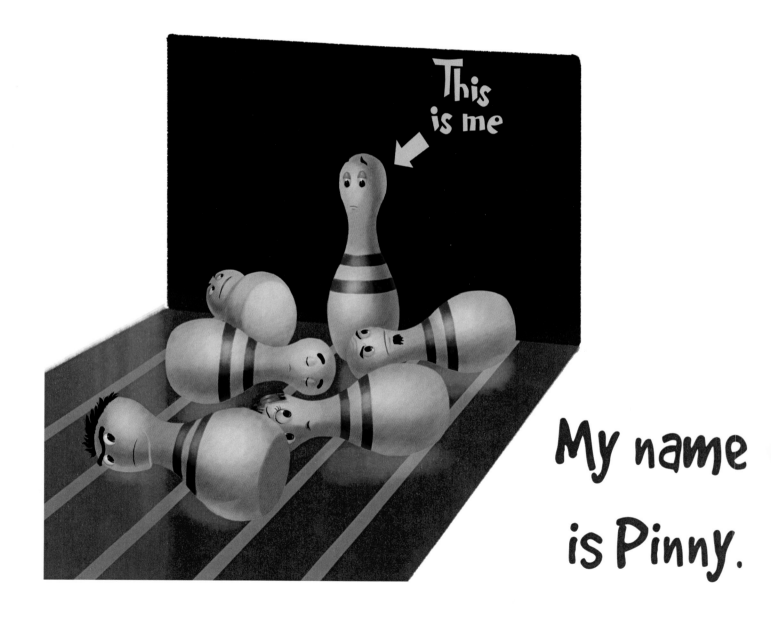

I'm a bowling pin.

Most of the time, I don't fall.

Which I know, makes people sad.
Everyone dislikes the last pin. Trust
me, it's disappointing
on my end too.

Maybe next
time dear..

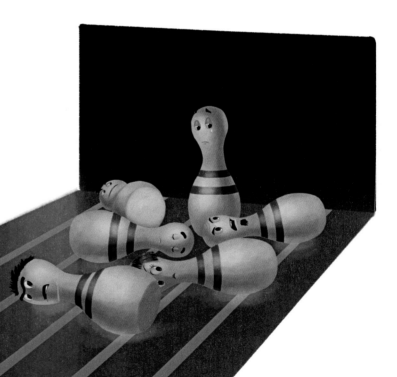

I must have a low center of gravity or something.

This is the line up, we rotate after every roll. I'm a backliner and one day, I'll be a frontliner, I know it!

Frontliners get all the action!

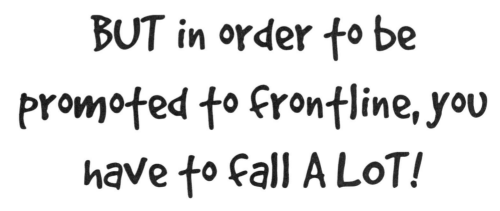

BUT in order to be promoted to frontline, you have to fall A LOT!

Which... Remember...
I sort of don't do very often.

Maybe I'm not meant to be just a bowling pin.
Maybe I want to do BIGGER things!

Or... Maybe I want to LIGHT up someone's world!

Or I could be a musician and rock the stage!

But, while I was daydreaming,

The ball zoomed right by me again!

Then Jock, the current frontliner, pushed my buttons.

But, maybe he's right...

Jock just kept being rude.

But, I wasn't listening to him.

That didn't stop him though, he became even meaner!

I didn't react the way he expected me to.

Which, made him really mad!

So, he did something pretty crazy next.

He pushed me!

And...

I fell down.

My boss saw me and
guess what?

He instantly promoted me to Jock's position!

Jock got moved to the backline.

And I was a FRONTLINER!

So maybe I was meant
to be a bowling pin!

And all I needed was a little push!

THE END.

Pinny
the Bowling Pin

27269074R00020

Made in the USA
San Bernardino, CA
27 February 2019